TO LEARN MORE

AT THE LIBRARY

Bowman, Chris. *Pickup Trucks.* Minneapolis, Minn.: Bellwether Media, 2018.

Mack, Larry. *Honda Ridgeline.* Minneapolis, Minn.: Bellwether Media, 2019.

Mack, Larry. *Toyota Tacoma.* Minneapolis, Minn.: Bellwether Media, 2019.

ON THE WEB

Learning more about the Nissan Frontier is as easy as 1, 2, 3.

1. Go to www.factsurfer.com.
2. Enter "Nissan Frontier" into the search box.
3. Click the "Surf" button and you will see a list of related web sites.

With factsurfer.com, finding more information is just a click away.

INDEX

The images in this book are reproduced through the courtesy of: Nissan, front cover (hero), pp. 2-3 (truck), 4-5, 6-7, 8, 10, 12-13, 14-15, 16-17, 18-19, 19, 20-21, 21 (left, middle, right); Andrey Kuzmin, front cover (title texture), pp. 7 (metal), 9 (metal), 10 (metal), 15 (metal), 20 (metal); Cyrustr, front cover (background); xpixe, front cover (top mud, bottom mud); diogoppr, front cover (mud splash); tanuha2001, pp. 2-3 (logo); Yulia Plekhanova, pp. 2-3 (background); USARJ NCO CORPS/ Flickr, p. 9; Bull-Doser/ Wikipedia, p. 11; Rodrigo Garrido, p. 15; sociologas, p. 21 (metal).

TOUGH TRUCKS

NISSAN FRONTIER

BY LARRY MACK

TORQUE™

BELLWETHER MEDIA • MINNEAPOLIS, MN

Are you ready to take it to the extreme? Torque books thrust you into the action-packed world of sports, vehicles, mystery, and adventure. These books may include dirt, smoke, fire, and dangerous stunts.
WARNING read at your own risk.

This edition first published in 2019 by Bellwether Media, Inc.

Library of Congress Cataloging-in-Publication Data

LC record for Nissan Frontier available at https://lccn.loc.gov/2018003586

Editor: Betsy Rathburn Designer: Josh Brink

Printed in the United States of America, North Mankato, MN.

TABLE OF CONTENTS

MOUNTAIN ROADS

The driver steers the pickup along a mountain road. It is a difficult ride full of twists and curves.

But the driver is not worried. His Nissan Frontier can handle it. This tough truck was designed for tricky roads!

The driver starts up a steep slope. Computers in the Frontier control the brakes. This stops the truck from rolling backwards. It also lets the driver focus on steering.

ANOTHER NAME

IN EUROPE AND ASIA, THE NISSAN FRONTIER IS CALLED THE NISSAN NAVARA.

The Nissan Frontier is both **rugged** and smart. People love this popular pickup!

NISSAN FRONTIER HISTORY

The Nissan Motor Company started in Japan in 1933. In four years, the company released its first **mass-produced** vehicle. The Datsun Type 15 turned heads!

Datsun 15 Roadster

WHAT'S IN A NAME?

THE NAME NISSAN COMES FROM THE JAPANESE WORDS *NIHON SANGYO*. THIS MEANS "JAPANESE INDUSTRY."

Building more cars meant Nissan could lower prices. More people could afford their vehicles! By **World War II**, the company began making trucks for the Japanese army.

In 1958, Nissan started selling cars in the United States. The next year, the first Datsun pickup truck was sold in the United States. Nissan pickups became very popular in the 1980s!

1964 Datsun 1200 Deluxe

DATSUN TRUCKS

UNTIL 1986, NISSAN SOLD ITS CARS AND TRUCKS UNDER THE DATSUN NAME.

1998 Nissan Frontier

In 1997, the company introduced the Nissan Frontier. It was soon Nissan's top-selling truck. It became so popular that Nissan later moved Frontier **production** to the United States.

NISSAN FRONTIER TODAY

The Nissan Frontier is a midsize pickup. It can tow up to 6,710 pounds (3,043 kilograms). It can pull heavy trailers, campers, and boats!

The inside of the Frontier **cab** is cool, too. Modern gadgets make the truck fun and safe for drivers and passengers. It is the perfect pickup for city streets and rough dirt roads!

FEATURES AND TECHNOLOGY

Nissan Frontier Midnight Edition

The Frontier is available in many **models**. One is the Desert Runner. It is for drivers who love adventure. It has special **suspension** designed for **off-road** driving.

RACE TRUCKS

NISSAN TRUCKS HAVE COMPETED AT FAMOUS RACES LIKE THE BAJA 1000, THE DAKAR, AND MANY OTHERS!

The Midnight Edition is just as tough as other Frontiers. But it also has attractive black features, like its grille and wheels. This styling helps make this special version look great on city streets.

Nissan Frontier Desert Runner

Some Frontiers have **four-wheel drive**. This feature sends power to all four wheels. The four-wheel drive and lightweight wheels help the Frontier handle sand, mud, and snow!

A Frontier has a king cab or a crew cab. Both have a room for three passengers behind the driver. Both also have four doors instead of two. But the king cab has more room!

The Frontier is full of cool electronic features. Some trucks come with a stereo that has ten speakers!

Drivers can hook up their smartphones to the pickup. This leaves their hands free so that they can drive more safely. There is even an app that will read text messages out loud!

2018 NISSAN FRONTIER SV V6 SPECIFICATIONS

ENGINE	4.0L V6 ENGINE
HORSEPOWER	261 HP (195 KILOWATTS) @ 5,600 RPM
TORQUE	281 LB-FT (39 KG-M) @ 4,000 RPM
TOWING CAPACITY	UP TO 6,710 POUNDS (3,044 KILOGRAMS)
MAXIMUM PAYLOAD	UP TO 1,430 POUNDS (649 KILOGRAMS)
FUEL ECONOMY	15 TO 23 MILES PER GALLON
CURB WEIGHT	UP TO 4,326 POUNDS (1,962 KILOGRAMS)
WHEEL SIZE	16 INCHES (41 CENTIMETERS)

TRUCK OF THE FUTURE

The Nissan Frontier has an exciting future. New **generations** are sure to have updated features. Some experts think it will have a sportier look.

Whatever Nissan decides, the Frontier is sure to remain popular. This little pickup has the power to get tough jobs done!

TOP SELLER

NISSAN AND ITS PARTNER COMPANIES MAY HAVE BEEN THE WORLD'S LARGEST AUTOMAKER IN 2017. THEY SOLD OVER 10 MILLION VEHICLES!

HOW TO SPOT A NISSAN FRONTIER

ROUNDED HOOD

ANGLED HEADLIGHTS

SLEEK BODY

GLOSSARY

cab—the area of a pickup where the driver and passengers sit

four-wheel drive—a feature that allows the engine to turn all four wheels at once

generations—versions of a model

mass-produced—built in large numbers

models—specific kinds of trucks

off-road—taking place on unpaved roads

production—the building of something

rugged—strong in character

suspension—springs and shocks that help a car grip the road

World War II—a conflict from 1939 to 1945 that involved many of the world's countries